Sticky People

by TONY JOHNSTON

Illustrated by CYD MOORE

HarperCollins Publishers

Library of Congress Cataloging-in-Publication Data

Johnston, Tony.

  Sticky people / by Tony Johnston ; illustrated by Cyd Moore.—1st ed.

    p.   cm.

  Summary: Sticky children playfully spread their stickiness around until bathtime changes everything.

  ISBN-10: 0-06-028759-4 — ISBN-10: 0-06-028760-8 (lib. bdg.)

  ISBN-13: 978-0-06-028759-7 — ISBN-13: 978-0-06-028760-3 (lib. bdg.)

  [1. Cleanliness—Fiction. 2. Baths—Fiction. 3. Stories in rhyme.] I. Moore, Cyd, ill. II. Title.

PZ8.3.J639St 2006   2003014357

[E]—dc22

Typography by Neil Swaab

1 2 3 4 5 6 7 8 9 10

First Edition

For Levi and Jamie
—T. J.

For Brooklyn, my little sticky neighbor
—C. M.

Sticky people, sticky people,
That is who they are.
Faces full of purple jelly
Shine like purple stars.

Sticky people eat their breakfast
In their sticky seats.
Waffles, pancakes, maple syrup,
Nothing that is neat.

Sticky people crawl around in
Little sticky pants,
In and out of flower gardens,
Making friends with ants.

Sticky people love to play with
Furry teddy bears.
Fuzzy, wuzzy, sticky also.
No one sticky cares.

Sticky people give tea parties
In their party jeans,
Slurping, burping daintily like
Sticky kings and queens.

Gloopy people, soupy people
Run outside to play
Hide-and-seek and seek-and-hide. They
Sneak around all day.

Sticky people love the mud, such
Goopy-oopy-ooze.
They scoop it, floop it into mud cakes
With their little shoes!

Sticky people rub their noses.
It's a funny trick,
Seeing if together they can
Make their noses stick.

Sticky people drag red wagons
Up and down the lawn,
Piling all their glicky friends in.
Everyone sticks on!

Flopsy people, dropsy people
Coming home once more.

"Hello, darling precious pumpkin!"
Look who's at the door.

Sticky people cozy up for
Stories in warm laps.
Sticky listeners suck their thumbs and
Snore their sticky naps.

Sticky people wake and yawn. They
Snack on nice ice cream.
Licky people, licky people,
That is what they seem

To little dogs and little cats who
Love them, goodness knows.
Love their faces, love their fingers,
Love their chocolate toes.

Sticky people dibble-dabble
With good gooey glue.
They make lovely sticky cards for
Grammas to stick to.

Dribbly people, bibbly people
Dine in fancy hats,
Squeezing mashed potatoes into
Mashed-potato cats.

Sticky people, sticky people
Take a bubbly bath.
"Look who's underneath that gunk!" their
Scrubbing fathers laugh.

Bubbly people, scrubbly people,
Clean as rubber ducks.
Droopy mothers, droopy fathers
Hug and kiss and tuck

Shiny people, shiny people
And their teddies in—

Till tomorrow, when they'll get all
Stickied-up again.